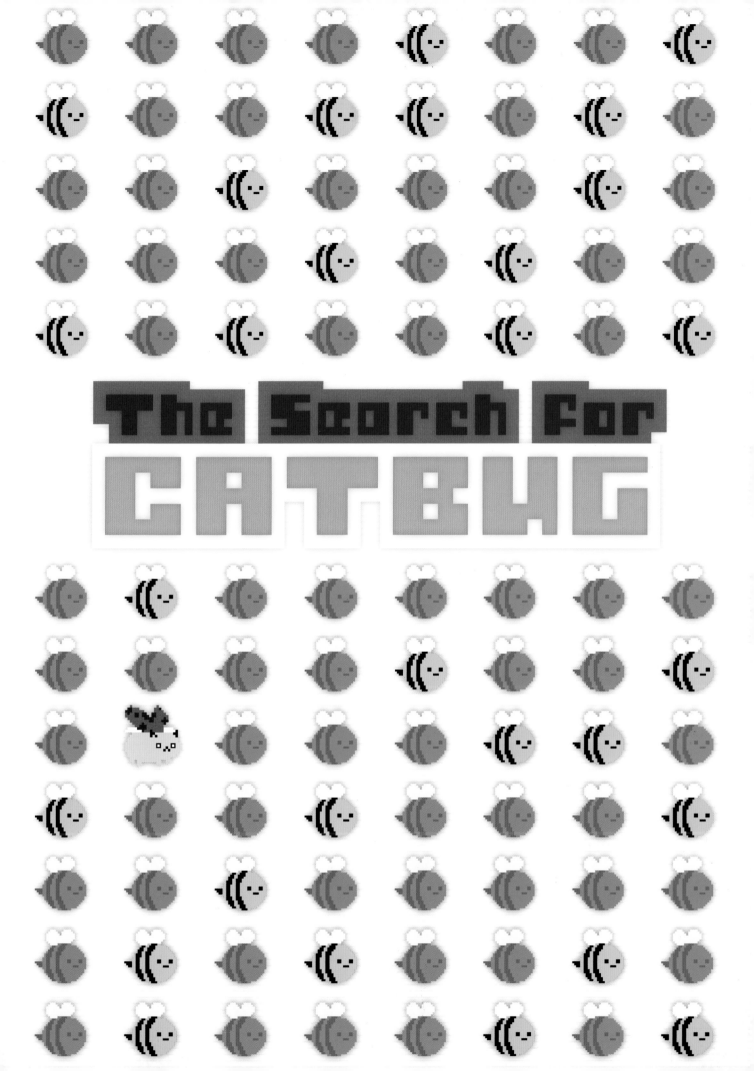

CARTOON HANGOVER
BRAVEST WARRIORS

What's happened to CATBUG?!

Writer ›› Joel Enos   Artist ›› Alan Brown

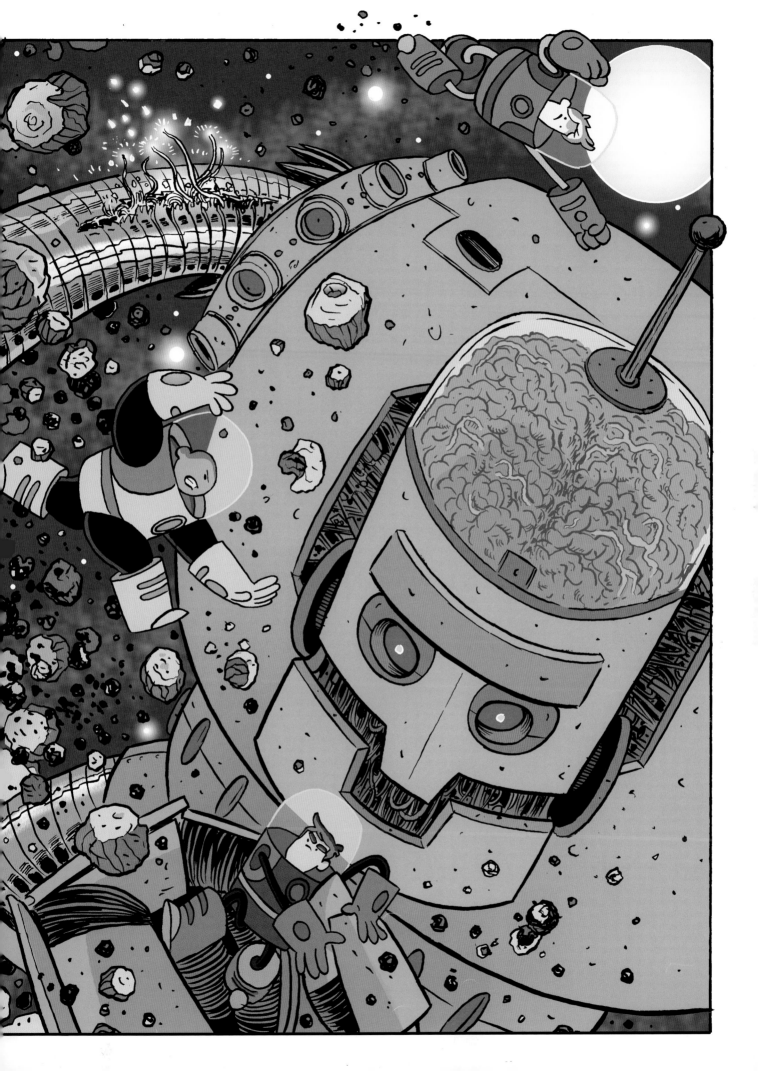

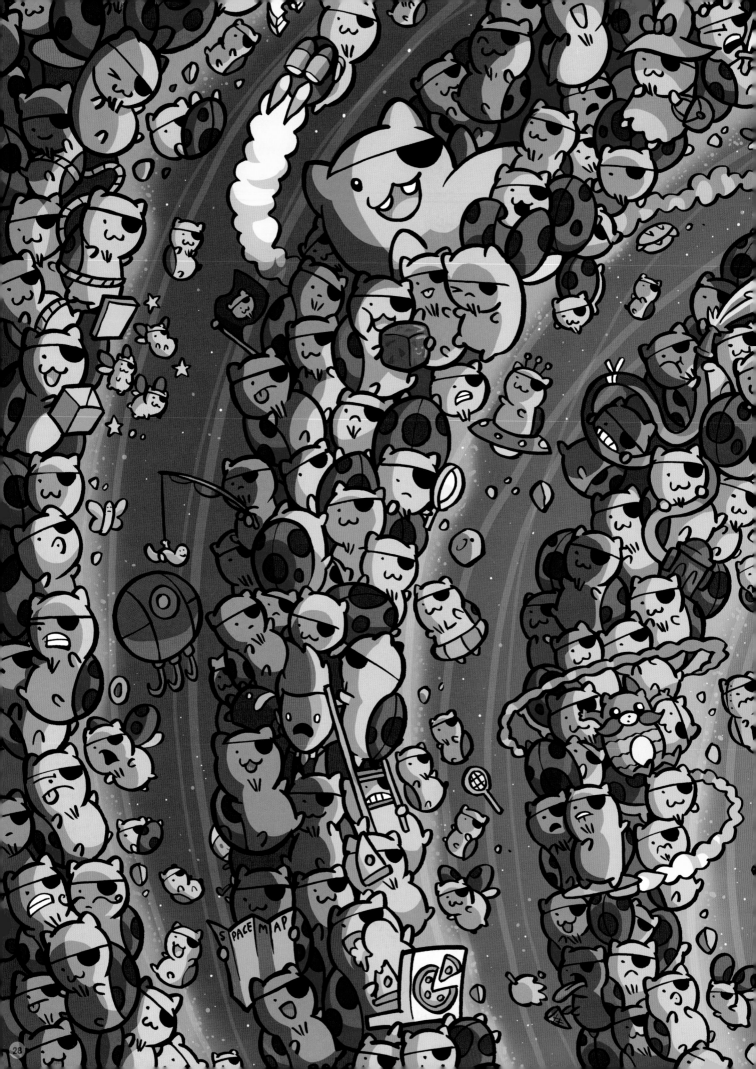

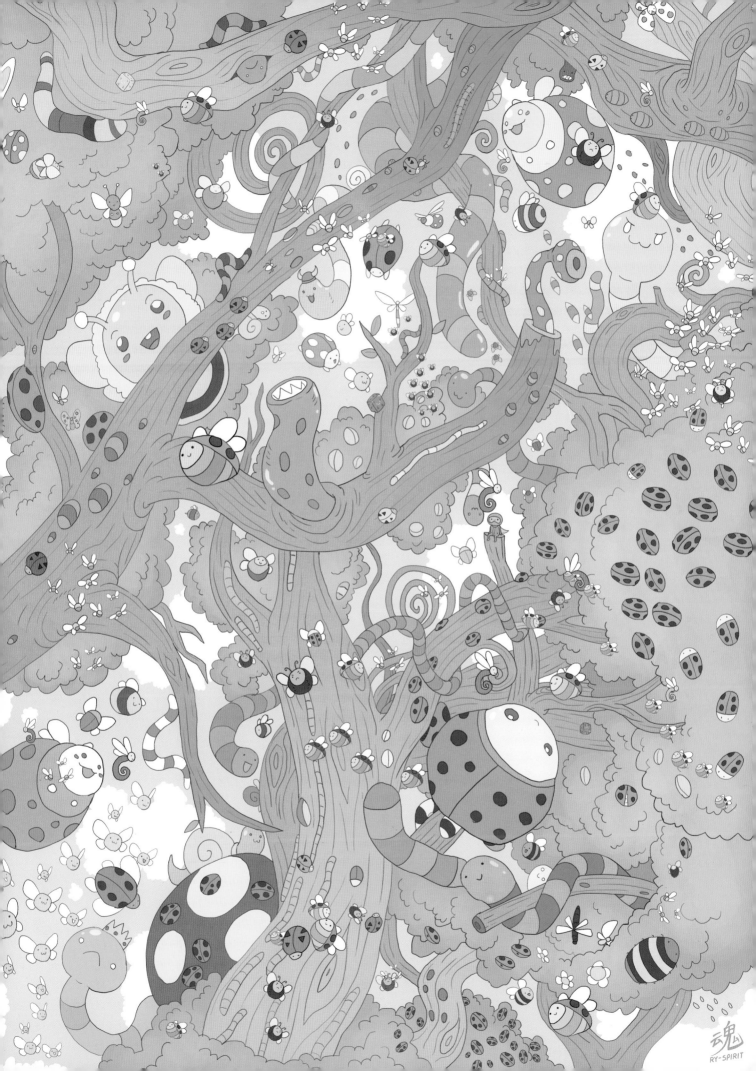

THE ARTISTS
+ANSWER KEY

ALAN BROWN
pp04-05

RACHAEL HUNT
pp06-07

MR. WARBURTON
pp08-09

ZACK TURNER
pp10-11

DAN CIURCZAK
+ JR ROBINSON [COLORS]
pp12-13

BECCA HILLBURN
pp14-15

CORIN HOWELL
pp16-17

JORGE CORONA
pp18-19

NATE LOVETT
pp20-21

BRIAN SMITH
pp22-23

IAN MCGINTY
+ FRED C. STRESING [COLORS]
pp24-25

LEE FERGUSON
+ ZACK TURNER [COLORS]
pp26-27

JAMIE SMART
pp28-29

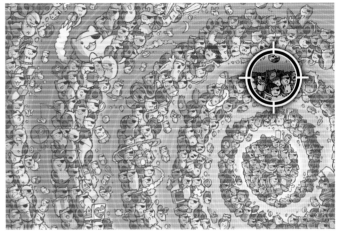

JORGE MONLONGO
pp30-31

ANDY HIRSCH
pp32-33

ANGAEL DAVIS
pp34-35

STU LIVINGSTON
pp36-37

JAN WIJNGAARD
pp38-39

MAURIZIO CAMPIDELLI
pp40-41

RY-SPIRIT
pp42-43

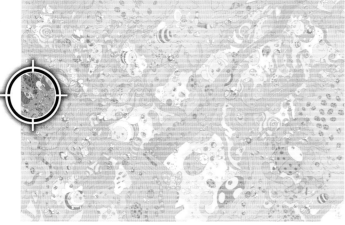

SAMANTHA C
pp44-45

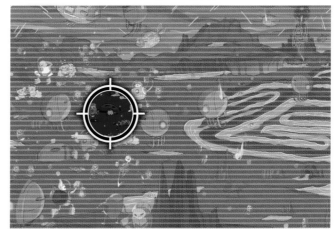

MATT CUMMINGS
pp46-47

JEREMY KUHN
pp48-49

SONIA LEONG
pp50-51

INORI FUKUDA TRANT
pp52-53

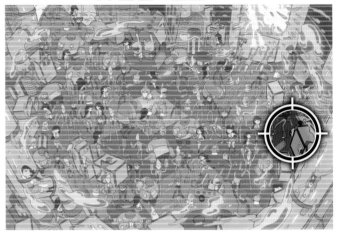

JON CHAO
pp54-55

MAD RUPERT
+ ZACK TURNER [COLORS]
pp56-57

DOMO STANTON
pp58-59

JOEL ENOS
EDITOR

Bravest Warriors, The Search for Catbug

Editor ›› **Joel Enos**   Design ›› **Fawn Lau**
Senior Editorial Director ›› **Elizabeth Kawasaki**

SPECIAL THANKS to **Jesse DeStasio**, **Eric Homan**, **Nate Olson**,
Chris Troise and the team at **Frederator**

Printed in China

Published by VIZ Media, LLC   Perfect Square Edition
P.O. Box 77010   10 9 8 7 6 5 4 3 2 1
San Francisco, CA 94107   First Printing, August 2014